PUFFIN BOO

Editor: Kaye Webb

PS 203

ROM-BOM-BOM AND OTHER STORIES

Here are nine perfect animal stories for reading aloud to children under seven. Many of them were originally written for broadcasting, and all of them have that happy combination of robust good humour, entertaining story, and rhythmic handling of words which has made Antonia Ridge one of the most popular and skilful authors for younger children.

'Rom-bom-bom', the title story, is about a jolly little lamb who evaded the clutches of his enemies by rolling home in a drum. 'F. Coconut, Esquire' is about an ordinary boy and his extraordinary dog who spend one morning flying round the town delivering the milk. The time the stories take to read will depend on the number of times the reader pauses to look at Ralph Thompson's charming illustrations, but all of them will delight and satisfy their audience.

ROM-BOM-BOM

and other stories

BY ANTONIA RIDGE

Illustrated by Ralph Thompson

PENGUIN BOOKS

Penguin Books Ltd, Harmondsworth, Middlesex, England
Penguin Books Inc., 3300 Clipper Mill Road, Baltimore, Md 21211, U.S.A.
Penguin Books Australia Ltd, Ringwood, Victoria, Australia

—

First published by Faber & Faber 1946
Published in Puffin Books 1963
Reprinted 1965, 1968

—

—

Made and printed in Great Britain
by Cox & Wyman Ltd,
London, Fakenham and Reading
Set in Monotype Baskerville

CONTENTS

ROM-BOM-BOM

THERE was once a jolly little lamb, who went about enjoying himself very much indeed. He frisked merrily round on his nimble little legs, and even when he stopped from time to time to take a little meal, he only

nibbled the very nicest, tenderest grass, so I can truthfully say he never really stopped enjoying himself all day long.

One day he was feeling even brighter and merrier than ever, and he said to himself, 'I think I'll go and see my Grannie. That's what I'll do! I'll go and see my Grannie. Baa-aa, what a clever little lamb I am to think of a good idea like that. All by myself too, baa-aa. Oh, baa-aa, won't I just enjoy myself!' And he jumped off all four legs at once in the most joyful way. You see, his Grannie was the very nicest sort of grannie, and he knew she simply loved seeing him romping round enjoying himself. And when he thought of all his Grannie's lovely meals, breakfast, dinner, tea, AND SUPPER, he jumped high in the air again and laughed out loud, 'Baa-haa-ha-ha!' And off he gambolled, singing merrily:

> *'Oh, what fun to be a lamb, lamb, lamb,*
> *And go and see your Gran, Gran, Gran!'*

And then, dear, oh dear, he came face to face with a fox! A very greedy fox, who enjoyed nothing better than gobbling up a tender little lamb. The fox looked at him and said in a hungry, disappointed voice:

> *'Hm, I s'pose you'll do for my din-din-din,*
> *Though you're very small and thin-thin-thin!'*

'Oh yes, Sir, I am,' agreed the clever little lamb:

> *'But I'm off to my Gran's to get fat-fat-fat,*
> *I'll be lovely to eat like that-that-that!'*

And so the greedy fox agreed to let the little lamb go to his Grannie's and get nice and fat.

But would you believe it, before he'd gone very far he met a tiger!

And then a wolf!

And then a lion!

And they were all very, very hungry, and they all loved tender little lambs for dinner. However, the little

lamb politely pointed out how thin and small he was, and added obligingly:

> '*But I'm off to my Gran's to get fat-fat-fat,*
> *I'll be just lovely to eat like that-that-that!*'

And so, one after the other, they sensibly agreed to let the little lamb go off to his Grannie's and get nice and fat.

At last the little lamb, quite safe and sound, came skipping up to his Grannie's front door, and oh, how glad she was to see him!

'Baa-aa, Grannie dear,' said our honest little lamb.
'I've promised faithfully to stay with you until I'm nice
and fat. And so of course I must keep my word.' And he
took another big helping of his Grannie's nice supper.

'Quite right, maa-aa, quite right!' said his Grannie
with loving pride.

And when he couldn't eat another mouthful the little
lamb said, 'Now, will you please lift me up into your
big wooden chest over there, for baa-aa, I'd better start
getting fat straight away.'

So his Grannie lifted him up into the big wooden
chest, and there he stayed for seven long days. And he
ate, and ate, and *ate*, and ATE, breakfasts, dinners, teas,
AND SUPPERS, as hard as he could go. And he grew

fatter and fatter, till even his Grannie was astonished, and she said, 'My goodness, you'd better go home now, little lamb.'

'Not I,' said the fat little lamb; 'the tiger will eat me up!'

'But,' said his Grannie, beginning to look very worried indeed, 'everybody's got to go home some time or the other. And I think you'd better go now, before you get too fat to walk.'

'All right then,' said our fat little lamb. 'But first of all listen carefully, Grannie, and I'll tell you what to do.'

So his Grannie listened carefully. And then she went out and bought a fine large goatskin, and she stretched it, and she stitched it, and she made it into a BEAUTI- FUL DRUM. The little lamb curled comfortably up inside, and his kind Grannie gave him a loving pat, and then fixed on the top. It fitted perfectly. So his Grannie looked very pleased indeed, and she gave it a gentle push. And off rolled the drum! And as she watched it roll gaily out of sight she could hear the fat little lamb inside singing away:

> '*Oh, what fun to go rom-bom-bom,*
> *And roll off home in a drum-drum-drum!*'

And he rolled on and on, and by and by he rolled straight into the tiger. The tiger, who was hungrier than ever, roared:

> '*D-r-r-um, d-r-um, drum, where's that nice fat lamb*
> *Who's been to see his Gran-gran-gran?*'

And from his cosy nest the lamb called out:

'Rom-bom-bom! He's lost in the wood!
You won't eat him, he's gone for good!'

And off he rolled, singing very loudly:

'Rombom, rombom,
Rom-bom-bom!'

You should have seen that tiger's face! 'Why didn't
I eat him when I had the chance?' he growled angrily.
And from far, far away came a merry little echo:

'Rombom, rombom,
Rom-bom-bom!'

On and on rolled the drum, and presently it rolled
straight into the wolf.

And then into the lion!

And they roared fiercely, one after the other:

'D-r-r-um, d-r-um, drum, where's that nice fat lamb,
Who's been to see his Gran-gran-gran?'

And the lamb from his cosy nest called out:

'Rom-bom-bom! He's lost in the wood!
You won't eat him, he's gone for good!'

And they were both very, very angry because, as I've
said before, they *did* like a nice fat lamb for dinner.

And quite soon, rom-bom-bom, the drum rolled
straight into the fox, who called out in a polite, wheed-
ling voice:

'Have you met, dear drum, a nice fat lamb,
Who's been to see his Gran-gran-gran?'

And the little lamb shouted back gleefully:

'Rom-bom-bom! He's lost in the wood!
You won't eat him, he's gone for good!'

But the hungry fox was very smart and sly, and he at once recognized the little lamb's voice. So he raced up to the rolling drum and growled:

'I know you're there, with your rom-bom-bom,
So out you come from that drum-drum-drum.'

At this the lamb laughed out very loudly indeed, and

rolled off faster and faster, and though the fox ran and ran like the wind, he just couldn't catch up with the drum. And by and by he had to give up the chase. As he sat, panting and furious under a tree, from far, far away, he could hear the lamb singing merrily:

'Rom-bom-bom! Oh, rom-bom-bom!
Roll straight home, my drum-drum-drum.'

And of course he did roll safely home. Otherwise, however should I be able to tell you this story?

LITTLE KID MONDAY

THERE was once a very hard-working Mother Goat, with a fine thick coat as white as snow. She had a large family of children and all of them were snow-white too. This, of course, meant a great deal of work for Mother Goat, who was most particular and liked nothing better than to see her children frisking round in the sunshine, as clean and spotless a family of goats as anyone could ever wish to meet.

Now Mother Goat often used to declare that she was far too busy an animal to sit down and think out fancy names for all her children. She also said that, after all, they could choose their own names when they grew up, and that for the time being, as there were exactly seven of them, they might just as well be named after the days of the week. And as it was on a Tuesday that she first thought of this sensible idea, she straightway named her eldest child Tuesday.

And the next she called Wednesday.

And the next Thursday.

And then came Friday.

And then the twins, Saturday and Sunday.

And the youngest of them all she called little Kid Monday.

They lived in a neat little house on the side of a hill. It was a very clean little house indeed, for as I've mentioned before, Mother Goat was most particular. She got up early every morning, and she scoured and scrubbed, and rubbed and polished, till the house simply sparkled and shone both inside and out.

Then she would call the seven little goats, and sing as she stirred the porridge:

> 'Wake up, Thursday! Wake up Friday!
> All the house is clean and tidy.
> Tuesday, Wednesday, Saturday, Sunday,
> And you as well, dear little Kid Monday.
> Come, clean your teeth and brush your hair,
> White goats should be clean and fair.'

Then up would jump the seven little goats, and clean their teeth, and help each other to brush and comb their thick white coats. And you may be sure that all the while Mother Goat kept a very sharp eye on them, as well as on the porridge, so that by the time they sat down to breakfast they really did look most clean and fair. This made Mother Goat smile proudly all round the table as she served the porridge, and sliced the bread, and spread the honey.

Sometimes she would wipe her eyes on the corner of her spotless apron and sigh, 'Oh, maa-aa, if only your dear Paa-aa could see you now!' She would then go on to tell the little goats all about their Paa-aa, who was, it seemed, a soldier, brave and bold, and the pride of his regiment, so that he always marched in front of his men, in a splendid coat of red and gold, as fine and handsome a goat as ever served his King and Country.

Here little Kid Monday would bang hard on the table with his spoon and shout very loudly that he was going to be a soldier one day too, and march alongside his Paa-aa, that he would, they'd see if he wouldn't. At this Mother Goat would look at him very hard, and say in a quiet voice, 'Well, we'll just see how brave you are on Friday.'

You see, Friday night was bath-night, and little Kid Monday simply hated having a bath. He always kicked, and splashed, and roared, and complained that the water was too hot, or too cold, and that the soap was up his nose or in his eyes, or even both. In short, he was a very bad naughty kid in his bath.

But then when he was dried and brushed and combed, he used to look so beautiful and clean, standing there in front of the kitchen fire, saying how sorry he was, and how he'd never, never do it again that his Maa-aa always forgave him on the spot. Though mind you, she often and often said what a mercy it was his brothers and sisters never kicked up such a fuss, but stood there as good as gold, bless their hearts, while she scrubbed and rubbed them as snowy clean as best yellow soap and warm water could make them.

18

At which, I'm sorry to say, little Kid Monday would mutter naughty things inside himself, such as: 'Best yellow soap! Huh! Worst of all yellow I should say! Soap and water! Huh!' He also began to think how very nice it would be if a clever young goat such as he could think out a plan to stop all soap and water, and so put an end to bath-nights for ever.

However, he soon saw it was no use thinking about water. There was simply gallons and gallons of it in the well in the garden, not to mention the brook that ran through the wood.

But soap now! Perhaps a clever young goat could manage something about soap –

Well, one Wednesday morning, that naughty little goat came scampering out of the house, simply dancing with glee. And when he was a long, long way away, where no one could hear, he jumped off all four legs at once, and began to sing:

> '*Oh, no more soap for me, for me!*
> *I've hid it all where Maa-aa can't see!*
> *Oh, jump and shout and laugh hee-hee,*
> *No more baths for me, for me!*'

This, of course, explains why the very next Friday morning, Mother Goat, looking very puzzled and upset, was heard to bleat, 'Now whatever did I do with all my soap? Six big bars of very best yellow. Oh, maa-aa, wherever can they be?' But though she hunted high, and she hunted low, she couldn't find her soap anywhere at all.

So at last she said she supposed she'd better go straight off to market and buy some more, and that they were all to be as good as gold and go indoors to their supper the minute the sun sank over the tall fir tree in the wood. And big sensible Kid Tuesday was to be sure and lock and bolt the door and not open it to anyone at all till she came home. 'For,' said poor Mother Goat, 'it's a weary way to the market, and I may not be home till late.'

Somehow, little Kid Monday didn't feel so happy as all that as he and the others waved their Maa-aa goodbye from the top of the hill, even though he kept telling himself that there would be no nasty wet baths that night at any rate. And for the first time in his young life he was quite glad when the sun began to set over the wood, and they all went indoors to supper.

Kid Tuesday very carefully locked and barred the door, but he'd hardly served the bread and milk, when, clop-clop, there came a loud knock on the door. 'Hurrah! Hurrah!' shouted all the little goats with one accord, 'It's Maa-aa! It's Maa-aa come back with the soap!'

And from outside a rough voice roared:

'Yes, that's right. It's your Maa-aa with the soap.
Come, open the door. You've been good I hope.'

Now there was something very strange about that gruff voice, something that made the little goats sit quite still and look at each other.

So presently the rough voice roared again:

'Come, open the door! Do as you're told.
Don't dare leave your Maa-aa out in the cold!'

At this, clever little Kid Monday called out:

'You're not our Maa-aa. Her voice is sweet.
You're the bad old wolf hunting for meat.'

When he heard this, the wolf, very angry, rushed straight off home. (Oh yes, it really was the wolf.)
And he gargled, and gargled, and gargled.
And very slowly he sipped a large glassful of black-currant tea.
And four large tablespoonfuls of honey.
Then he went softly back, and rapped on the door, and called out in a smooth, honeyed voice:

'Now open the door, children dear.
It's your Maa-aa this time as you can hear.'

But before the others could jump out of bed, little **Kid**
Monday ran and peeped under the door. And my, oh
my, what did he see but four black legs, standing there
in the moonlight. So he shouted loud and clear:

> '*Oh wicked paws as black as night,*
> *You're not our Maa-aa, she's snowy-white.*'

At this the angry wolf sped off home like the wind.
Grumbling fiercely, he soaked his feet and legs in warm

water, and rubbed and rubbed them with a large lump of chalk.

And very queer he looked too as he stole back through the silent night, his four chalky legs gleaming in the moonlight.

This time he gave a gentle tap-tap on the door and called in a soft, tired voice:

> '*Peep under the door, see paws so white.*
> *Fling back the bolt, it's your Maa-aa all right.*'

So with a shout of joy the little goats flung open the door.

And there, oh there, stood the wolf!

And dear, oh dear, how frightened they were!

Tuesday rushed behind the door.

Wednesday crept under the table.

Thursday got behind the bread-bin.

Friday jumped right inside the bread-bin.

Saturday and Sunday, poor little twins, crept under Maa-aa's rocking chair.

But where was Monday, little Kid Monday? Nobody knew. Not even the wicked wolf. But he found all the others, all six of them, and bundled them, one after the other, inside a large sack. Then he swung them on his back and swaggered off down the garden path, singing:

> '*Goats for supper, goats for tea,*
> *Oh, lovely treats in store for me!*'

But there at the gate, in a splendid red and gold coat, stood a soldier, armed to the teeth with a pistol, a sword, and a musket.

It was Sergeant-Major Paa-aa Goat, home on leave! 'Oho!' he roared, 'what's that on your back?'

And before the frightened wolf could answer **six** voices sang out:

'*Oh Paa-aa! It's us, we're all in the sack!*'

'That's right, Sir,' stuttered the wolf. 'I'm just taking them out for a treat. Just a little treat.'

'I'll treat you!' bellowed Paa-aa. 'I'll sack you! Oh,

my horns and sword, how I'll wallop and whack you!'

And he advanced with his sharp horns glittering like gold, and the light of battle blazing in his eyes.

But the wolf didn't wait. Oh, goodness, no! Spurred on by a mighty butt in the rear, he fairly flew over the garden gate just as Maa-aa came running up the lane bleating piteously, 'Oh Paa-aa, Paa-aa are they safe and sound?'

'Safe and sound,' roared back Paa-aa, 'in a sack on the ground.'

And he undid the sack and out crawled the little goats.

Oh my! Oh my! How glad they all were! How they skipped and danced around their Maa-aa and Paa-aa! And how they talked and talked as they trooped indoors.

Till suddenly Maa-aa gave a little bleat. 'But Paa-aa,' she cried, 'where is Monday, dear little Kid Monday? Wherever can he be?'

'Sh! Sh!' said Paa-aa sternly. They all stood still. And from the great tall grandfather clock in the kitchen, came a strange, strange song:

> '*Tick-tick-tock,*
> *In the clock.*
> *Tock-tock-tick*
> *Very sick.*
> *Oh, tock, oh, tick!*
> *Open quick.*'

Paa-aa flung open the door, and there inside the

clock, on six big bars of best yellow soap crouched little Kid Monday, looking very, very sorry for himself.

'Oh, poor, poor kid!' bleated Maa-aa, and she began to love and pet him.

But, 'Hi, you!' said Paa-aa very firmly. 'Attention! Forward march!' And he marched his youngest son out into the wood-shed, left-right-left-right, just like that.

Well, nobody will ever really know what happened there. All they know is that half an hour later Paa-aa and Kid Monday marched back into the kitchen again, arm in arm, as friendly as you please, and that Kid Monday was smiling and holding his head high in the air.

And all through supper, when everybody was laughing and talking and roaring at Paa-aa's merry jokes, it was only Maa-aa who noticed that Kid Monday was sniffing just a little, and that every now and then he would dab his eyes when he thought no one was looking.

But whatever was said or done in the wood-shed that night, it certainly worked wonders, for from that day to this you wouldn't find a better little goat than Kid Monday, no, not if you were to go all the way to Switzerland and back.

And what's more, his Maa-aa tells me he's a real pleasure to bath on a Friday night.

HENRY HORNBILL

MASTER HENRY BUCORVUS sat on a stout branch of a tree in the tall jungle, and sang and sang. His voice sounded something like the bray of a donkey and the shriek of a railway engine mixed together. But Henry liked his voice. In fact, he liked it very much indeed. So he sang and sang:

> '*I've got a bill, a lovely big bill.*
> *Oh, watch me juggle and eat my fill.*'

He rose heavily in the air on his great strong wings, and snapped off a fine bunch of berries from a near-by tree. And, whoops, he tossed them high in the air, caught them neatly in his wide-open bill as they fell, gave a little bow, and gobbled them all up! Just like that.

'My, oh my!' said his Grannie, old Mrs Hornbill, puffing her feathers out with pride. 'Henry has such nice manners!'

And she really meant it. Hornbills, you see, think it most polite to toss their food up in the air and catch it again before they eat it. That is of course why nobody ever dreams of telling you to go and play at being hornbills. Moreover I don't think I'd try if I were you in any case, because you really do need a most enormous beak as well as a great deal of practice.

Anyhow Henry wasn't singing and juggling with his

breakfast simply to please his Grannie. Oh no! I'm afraid he just loved showing off. For presently he flapped off his stout branch again and squawked:

> *'I've got wings, lovely strong wings,*
> *Oh, watch me fly and gobble up things.'*

And away he flew through the tall jungle, gobbling up insects like billy-oh. His wings made a fine chuffing, rushing noise, something like a very fussy train coming into a railway station. And Henry sang:

> *'Oh chuff, lovely wings, as I fly along,*
> *Oh chuff, chuff, chuff so loud and strong.'*

Then down he swooped to the river bank and juggled and gobbled a fat young snake. And feeling nice and full and very happy, he scrambled back on his branch again and made up another song:

> *'Oh, I've got eyes, lovely sharp eyes,*
> *I spy them all, snakes, fruit, and flies.'*

Just then to his surprise he heard a voice singing back:

> *'Oh, a bird like you, it seems to me,*
> *Should find a wife, well, just like me.'*

And up from a tree close by flapped a plump young hornbill. Her strong black wings shone in the warm sun. She made a wonderful noise like TWO goods trains steaming into a station as she churred along, catching insects like GREAT BILLY-OH in her huge, curved beak. And she swooped down to the river bank and juggled and gobbled TWO fine, fat snakes in the

smartest way. And then she flopped back again on a stout branch near Henry and asked, 'Well whoops?' in the politest way.

Henry looked at her thoughtfully for a moment and then said, 'Not bad! Not bad at all.' And flopped down on the branch beside her.

Then began a lovely time for Henry and his new wife. They went flying and swooping and squawking through all the tall jungle, and their wings made a most remarkable noise exactly like three very busy steam engines. And they juggled and gobbled, and juggled and gobbled, snakes, fruit, and flies. And Grannie Hornbill said proudly, 'Well, I'll say this for Henry and that new wife of his, they really have the most excellent manners. And I've seen some smart juggling in my time, that I have. Runs in the family, as you might say.'

However, one fine day Henry's wife said very severely, 'Now, Henry, it's high time we settled down and brought up a family. We really must set to work and find a comfortable hollow tree in some pleasant spot. So you go that way and search, and I'll go this.'

'Oh, all right,' said Henry. But he didn't sound very pleased. And no wonder either, for his wife was most particular. This tree was too big and draughty, that tree was too small and stuffy, this one was too much in the open, that one was too far away from the rest of the family. But at last they found a tree that was just right, with a cosy-sized hollow high up in its trunk.

Now if Henry's wife had been fussy about her tree, I'm bound to admit she was not in the least particular about the nest she built inside it. Dear me, no!

She just pushed the dead twigs inside the hollow into a rough, untidy heap.

Then she pulled out a few of her feathers and piled them on top.

And then she sat down and squawked, 'Whoops!' in a very satisfied voice.

Henry peered down into the dark hollow. 'Oh, good!' he cried. 'Now don't you move. I'll be back in a minute.'

And off he went to the river bank. And you'll find it very hard to guess what he did next.

He made some mud, some lovely, stiff mud. This is of course another reason why nobody ever suggests a game of hornbills. And anyhow I can't tell you how Henry made his mud because it is a very special and secret hornbill recipe.

Well, bit by bit, beakful by beakful, he plastered up the hole in the hollow tree, but right down the middle he left a good long slit. And as he flew to and fro he hummed:

> *'With beautiful mud, bit by bit,*
> *I'll build my door with a nice long slit.'*

He really took a lot of pains about this slit. His wife squawked a great deal of good advice too, from her nest inside the hollow tree where she had been sitting all the while. So that by and by when the mud door was finished, she could push her bill through it as comfortably as you please without bothering to get up from her rough nest. Oh yes, she was most comfortable, sitting there in the warm, dark hollow of the tree.

But for Henry now, things began to be very different! No more lovely times chuffing round and showing off. No more lazy times sitting in the sun puffing his feathers out and making up happy songs.

No, he just worked, and worked, and worked!

You see, he not only had to feed his wife, but that clever, noble, unselfish bird took the trouble to pack all her food in little parcels, wrapped in a thin, rubbery sort of skin. I can't tell you how he managed this. Nobody can. It is another hornbill secret. But I do know that inside the little parcels he put nice bits of fruit and seeds and insects, and even tasty snacks of snake. Then when he had them all ready inside that useful beak of his, off he'd fly to their tree.

Sometimes his wife would have her beak sticking out through the slit, all ready for a meal. And she would be grumbling away like anything, asking Henry if it wasn't bad enough to be shut up there in the dark all day without having to wait for her meals, and where on earth had he been, and other cross questions.

But sometimes Henry had to rap on the door with his beak and squawk, 'Show a beak there! Dinner's ready!'

'All right! All right!' his wife would reply, very sharply. 'No need to kick up such a din.' And she would push her beak through the slit and open it wide for her dinner.

Then clever, patient Henry would cling to the rough bark of the tree with his strong, clawed feet, and jerk his nice little parcels one after the other into his wife's open beak. One, two, three, and sometimes even four. And straightway fly off and start on her supper.

Oh yes, it was a busy, busy time for Henry.

And of course he got thinner and thinner and thinner.

And inside the hollow tree, his wife got fatter and fatter and fatter.

She even shed all her old feathers and grew a fine new set.

But poor Henry grew shabbier and shabbier and shabbier. His wings now only made a noise like a very tired train shunting wearily up and down. And he never seemed to have a moment to make up songs, not even the very shortest ones. He was truly a poor, poor, tired hornbill.

However, one bright morning, one really lovely morning, as Henry was starting out in search of his

wife's breakfast, he heard a strange noise. It was somebody busily hammering and chipping. And there was
his wife briskly battering down the mud door with her
great strong beak.

'Whoops! Oh me! Oh my!' squawked Henry in great
excitement, as his wife squeezed through the hole she'd
made and flapped heavily towards him.

'Look!' she cried.

And through the battered mud door peeped a fluffy head, a small head with a very big beak. Two sharp, brown eyes blinked through long, sweeping lashes, and a tiny voice squeaked, 'Hi! Oh, whoops! I'm hungry!'

It was Master Bucorvus, junior, saying hullo to a strange, new world.

Then Henry, looking proudly at his fine new son, forgot how tired and worn he was, and burst into glad new song:

> *'Oh, whoop and shout and squawk with me,*
> *I've got a son up in my tree.'*

And in less than no time all the hornbills in the tall jungle had heard him, and were joining in the joyful chorus.

F. COCONUT, ESQUIRE

THIS is not the usual sort of story because it is all about a fairy who didn't even know he was a fairy until half past eight last Tuesday morning. Up to that very moment he'd always thought he was just an ordinary sort of boy called Billy. And everybody else thought he was just an ordinary sort of boy too, except his mother, and his dog, who was called Alfred. Of course they thought he was a very special sort of boy. But even they never dreamed he was a fairy. Not even Alfred, who is a very clever dog indeed, and only called Alfred because he once had an accident with some cakes.

Well, last Tuesday week Billy woke up very early, feeling most unusual. And it wasn't altogether because of the sun pouring in through his open window, or the happy thought that he and Alfred had another whole day's holiday stretching straight out before them. No, it was something different, something that made Billy want to laugh and shout and stand on his head, and make up songs to sing at the top of his voice. Songs like this:

> '*Oh, won't I climb some nice old trees*
> *In nice old clothes, just like these!*
> *Oh, nice old shirt,*
> *And nice old pants,*
> *And nice old shoes!*

Oh, nice old day for Alf and me,
As nice as any day could be!'

And as he scrambled down the stairs he had a queer feeling he could easily have flown down if he'd only wanted to. However, the moment he opened the kitchen door his mother said, 'Do run and see if the milk is coming, there's a good boy. Breakfast is nearly ready.'

So Billy forgot all about the flying feeling and galloped off down the garden path, with Alfred barking and prancing at his heels.

When they came to the corner of the road they sat down under Mr Sparkes's hedge and waited for the milk. A biggish sort of boy brings their milk. He has red hair and freckles and he calls Billy 'Nipper'.

So Billy calls him 'Ginger'.

And they both spend a lot of time and thought making up other remarks to shout at each other.

Now it was as he sat there at exactly half past eight that Tuesday morning that Billy first began to know he was a fairy. But he says I am to be sure and make it very, very clear that he was NOT a Cissy-looking fairy. No, he went on looking like an ordinary boy, but magic, all sorts of lovely magic came bubbling up inside him.

'Hi, you watch this!' he said to Alfred. And he twisted the third button of his nice old shirt. Instantly, out from his back sprang two neat strong wings, just like a Spitfire's! And with a beautiful whirr-rr he shot high in the air, straight up and over Mr Sparkes's hedge.

And he flew up the road.

And he flew down the road.

Zoom – zum – ! In less time even than that.

And he turned somersaults in mid-air.

And he flew upside-down.

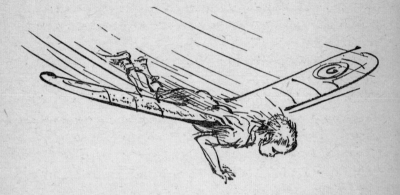

And right side down.

And he dived down low – z-z-z-Z-Z-Z.

And he shot up high again – Z-Z-Z-z-z-z.

Oh, it was simply grand.

And Alfred sat watching him, nearly bursting with pride.

'Wuff! Wuff!' he barked, as Billy swooped down beside him again and sent his wings neatly back by twisting his third button the other way. 'Oh, wuff! Oh, gosh! Why, you must be a fairy!'

'Seems like it,' said Billy, 'I've just sort of found it out. Seems I've got a new name too. It's F. Coconut, Esquire.'

(I happened to know why he chose this name. It was because of another wonderful moment last summer when he won a coconut with his very first shy, in front of a large and admiring crowd.)

'Oh, wuff!' said Alfred, absolutely delighted. 'Won't old Ginger get a shock!'

And at that very moment Ginger came round the corner, whistling and pushing his little cart.

'Hi-ya, Nipper!' he yelled. 'Come and get your nice milky-milky, my little man!'

'You!' said F. Coconut, Esquire, red with rage at these horrid words. 'You change into a cow.'

And he did.

A ginger-coloured cow, with large, brown, very surprised-looking eyes.

'Well, moo-oo!' said old Ginger.

'There!' said F. Coconut, Esquire. 'That'll teach you! Now you just follow me.'

And he began to push the little cart down the road, exactly as he'd always longed to do, only old Ginger would never hear of it. And Ginger and Alfred followed behind, sounding just like this:

'Well, moo-oo!'

'Wuff, wuff, oh, wuffetty-wuff!'

But they'd hardly gone any way when they met the girl from next door but one, the girl who says Alfred chases her cat and other unnecessary things.

'Oh, you'll catch it, pushing that cart,' she began. 'And oh, oh, oh, where did you get that horrid cow?' And she pretended to be very frightened.

'Moo-oo!' said old Ginger, most annoyed.

'Huh!' said F. Coconut, Esquire. 'You just mind your own business.'

'She won't! She never does!' barked Alfred. 'Better change her too!'

'All right,' said F. Coconut, Esquire. 'Here you, you change into something useful!'

And she did.

She changed into a most sensible little hen. 'Cluck, cluck,' she said, extremely pleased and satisfied. And she took up her place behind Ginger and Alfred.

42

Then off they went down the road again. And all the bottles of milk went click-click, left-right, left-right. And from behind came a cheerful chorus:

Moo-oo! Moo-oo!

Wuff, wuff! Oh, wuffetty-wuff!

Cluck, cluck! Oh, clucketty-cluck!

It was simply delightful.

And then they met Mr Sparkes going home to his breakfast. 'Well, well,' he called, as F. Coconut, Esquire, saluted and they all marched smartly past. 'Now, that's what I call a nice little turn-out and no mistake!'

F. Coconut, Esquire, was so pleased at this kind remark that he turned round and waved to Mr Sparkes and said softly, 'You change into something most important.'

And he did.

He changed into the Lord Mayor – with a real gold chain and a fine cocked hat.

'Well!' said Mr Sparkes. 'Now this is an honour and no mistake.'

'You're welcome,' said F. Coconut, Esquire. And they all stood still and watched Mr Sparkes hurry off to tell his wife.

'Attention!' said F. Coconut, Esquire. 'The time has now come to deliver the milk.'

He tapped two large bottles, and off they flew and set themselves down side by side on Mr Sparkes's door-step.

'Oh, wuff!' said Alfred.

'Oh, cluck!' said the hen.

And it was clear that they both thought this very clever indeed.

But, 'Moo-oo!' said old Ginger, in a most reproachful voice. 'One-one-one!'

'Oh, all right,' said F. Coconut, Esquire, going rather red. 'I know it only ought to be one, but Mrs Sparkes will be sure to want to celebrate.'

'Well, moo-oo!' said old Ginger, in a well-don't-let-it-happen-again voice.

'Now, you all watch this,' said F. Coconut, Esquire. And he twisted the third button of his nice old shirt. Out sprang his two neat strong wings, and off he flew with two quart bottles of milk.

And – zoom – ! He set one down on Miss Napper's doorstep.

And – zum – ! He flew over her hedge and set down the other one in Mrs Brown's porch.

'Oh, cluck, cluck!' said the hen, dancing up and

44

down in the greatest excitement as the flying milkman landed again.

'All right,' he said, 'you can try too. But only the half-pints mind! Steady now, steady!'

And away flew the sensible little hen, holding a small bottle tightly between her claws.

'Oh, ME too! Me too!' barked Alfred. And he sat up and began to beg.

So F. Coconut, Esquire, twisted the top button of his nice old shirt, and out shot two strong wings from the middle of Alfred's back. And off he flew with a pint bottle between his front paws, barking most joyously.

'Moo-oo, oh, moo-oo!' groaned old Ginger, breathing hard and looking most anxious.

'All right,' said F. Coconut, Esquire, kindly. 'You needn't fly. You just stay here and mind the cart.'

So old Ginger leaned happily against Mr Sparkes's hedge and watched them fly round with the milk.

Up and down the road they flew very steady and straight with the bottles, and set them down quietly on the doorsteps. But on the return journeys, my, oh my, what a time they had.

They played leap-frog over the chimneys.

They played hide-and-seek round the tops of the trees.

They flew flat on their backs.

They flew flat on their fronts.

It was simply wonderful.

But by and by, all the bottles of milk stood safe and sound on the right doorsteps.

And F. Coconut, Esquire, and Alfred, and the hen stood panting happily round the empty cart.

'Well,' said F. Coconut, Esquire, 'I suppose we'd better all change back now.'

And they did.

Old Ginger became a biggish sort of boy with red hair and freckles.

Alfred's wings gave a little click and vanished inside him.

The sensible little hen became the girl from next door but one again.

And F. Coconut, Esquire, became just an ordinary sort of boy called Billy.

'Well thanks, I'm sure,' said old Ginger. And off he went whistling and pushing his cart as if nothing had happened. But as he turned round the corner by Mr Sparkes's hedge he called back, 'Say, young Bill, you can give me a hand tomorrow too if you like.'

And the little girl skipped up and down on the pavement and said, 'Wasn't it lovely! Let me come to-morrow too, Billy!'

'All right,' said Billy. And he raced off home with Alfred at his heels.

As soon as he opened the kitchen door his mother looked up from the morning paper. 'Now, isn't that nice!' she said. 'Mr Sparkes is going to be our new Lord Mayor.'

'Yes, I know,' said Billy, and he sat down to his breakfast.

But somehow or another he wasn't at all certain why he knew. You see, being a fairy lasts for such a short time. And remembering about it lasts even less; but there, I expect you've already found that out for yourselves.

KICKING TREE

The Story of a Very Short Giraffe

THERE was once a very tall Father Giraffe, and a nearly-as-tall Mother Giraffe. They roamed happily round in the warm sunshine, and ate the topmost leaves of the tallest trees for their breakfasts, dinners, teas, and suppers.

By and by they had a baby son, with soft dark eyes and a skin like velvet.

And his Mother looked at him, and loved him. But she thought he looked just a little odd.

And his Father looked at him, and loved him. But he thought he looked just a little queer.

And so did his Grannie,

And his Grandpa.

And his Auntie.

And his Uncle.

And his big cousin Jo.

But they none of them said so, because giraffes never talk. They only think.

Then Father Giraffe leaned the baby against a tree, and they all stood back and looked at him. And he almost seemed part of the tree itself, so perfect was the pattern of light and shade on his velvet coat.

So they had another good look at him.

His Mother counted his legs.

His Grannie looked at his tongue.
His Grandpa looked at his eyes.
His Auntie looked at his ears.
His Uncle looked at his hoofs.
And his cousin Jo looked at his tiny horns.
And his legs, and his tongue, and his eyes, and his ears, and his hoofs, and his tiny horns, were all quite perfect.

Yet still they thought there was something queer.

So his cousin Jo galloped off like the wind, and came back with their neighbour, the black and white Ostrich.

The Ostrich looked at the baby giraffe, and he shut his eyes up tight, and buried his head deep down in the sand.

This made Mother Giraffe very cross. She swung her long neck sideways and gave the Ostrich a hard smack with her head.

The Ostrich pulled his head out, turned quickly

round, and raced off home like an express train. And as he ran, he gasped:

> '*Sorry, Jo!*
> *I do not know.*
> *I cannot tell.*
> *I've had a shock,*
> *I don't feel well.*'

Then Jo galloped off again, and this time he came back with the stripy Zebra.

And as soon as he saw the baby giraffe, the Zebra began to laugh, 'Qua-ha-ha, qua-ha-ha! Just look at his neck! Oh, qua-qua-ha!'

So they looked at his neck.

AND IT WAS SHORT.

VERY, VERY SHORT.

'Well,' said the stripy Zebra, 'don't stand staring at him. Try rubbing him in . . . or something!'

And he raced off, laughing and singing:

'Oh, qua-ha-ha! Qua-hee-hee!
Such a short giraffe I never did see!'

Then Father Giraffe leaned the baby against a tree again.

And Mother Giraffe made two marks on its trunk to show how long his neck was.

And on Mondays, his Father rubbed his neck with palm oil.

On Tuesdays, his Mother rubbed him with juice from the sugar cane.

On Wednesdays, his Grannie rubbed him with honey . . . lots of it.

On Thursdays, his Grandpa rubbed him with melon-juice.

On Fridays, his Auntie rubbed him with orange-juice.

And on Saturdays, his Uncle rubbed him with castor-oil.

And as soon as their backs were turned, the baby giraffe licked it all off with his lovely long tongue. He liked everything except the castor-oil. So he spat that out. And found a good place to hide in when Saturdays came round.

Every Sunday they leaned him against the tree to see how much his neck had grown.

And it did grow, but very, very slowly.

So that by the time he was five years old the baby

giraffe could just reach the very lowest branches of the tall trees if he stood on tiptoe. This would be very tall for you or me. But it's very, very short for a giraffe aged five.

And every time he galloped by, the stripy Zebra called out, 'Well, how's young Shorty? Qua-ha-ha!'

But of course nobody ever answered him. Giraffes never answer anybody. They just go on thinking.

Well, by and by, even Mother Giraffe began to think of her son as Shorty, and gave up worrying about his neck.

And they roamed happily round among the tall trees.

Father Giraffe ate the leaves of the topmost branches.

Mother Giraffe ate the leaves of the middle branches.

And Shorty ate the leaves of the lowest branches. But he still had to stand on tiptoe.

Then one night, Father Giraffe and Shorty went down to the pool to have a drink. Father Giraffe drank first. He stretched his front legs wide apart to bring his head down low to the water. And he drank and drank and drank. And Shorty leaned against a tree and watched him.

Suddenly there was a low rustle in the bushes.

And there in the moonlight stood a lion!

Shorty saw him plainly. But the Lion didn't see Shorty. He only saw Father Giraffe, with his head down low in the water, drinking and drinking.

And he smiled and licked his lips, and crouched back low to give a mighty spring.

And at that very moment, somebody behind him kicked and kicked.

My, oh my, was that Lion startled!

Over he rolled, straight into the water.

And like a flash Father Giraffe swung his head sharply sideways and whacked and walloped him. Whack! Whop! Whack!

How that Lion roared and spluttered! He scrambled
to the bank and flew off home like the wind, howling:

> *'Gr-rr-rr-rick!*
> *A trick! A trick!*
> *Oh, wicked tree*
> *To kick and kick!'*

And he made up his angry mind to catch Father
Giraffe, come what may, the very next day.

So the very next day, when the sun was low in the
sky, the Lion stole silently out.

He hid himself in a tangle of bushes and waited,
with his eyes fixed on the tops of the tallest trees.

Presently he saw two short horns sticking out above
the topmost branches. And he growled with glee:

> *'Grr-rr-rr! He won't see me,*
> *With head high up in tallest tree.'*

And he slunk from shadow to shadow till he could see
the back of Father Giraffe.

Father Giraffe couldn't see the Lion of course. He was
quietly eating his supper, with his head high up in the
tree.

But somebody else saw the Lion . . . somebody who
stood so still under another tree that he looked like part
of the tree itself . . . somebody too short to reach the topmost branches . . . somebody with eyes as sharp as
needles. . . .

And he waited till the Lion crept softly by. Then out
flashed his strong back legs, and he kicked, and kicked,
and kicked.

Down came Father Giraffe's long neck from the tall tree. From side to side he swung his hard head, and hammered, and hammered, and hammered.

Up ran Mother Giraffe with fiery eyes, to join in the fight.

And off flew the Lion, howling with terror:

> *'Away, away,*
> *I'll flee, I'll flee,*
> *From hammering head,*
> *And kicking tree.'*

And the Zebra, who had watched all this from a safe place, laughed loud and long:

> *'Qua-ha-ha!*
> *Qua-hee-hee!*
> *No more giraffe*
> *He'll hunt for tea.'*

He was right. That Lion never came back.

So all day long, tall Father Giraffe and nearly-as-tall Mother Giraffe and a not-nearly-as-tall young Giraffe roam happily round in the warm sunshine, eating the leaves of the tall trees.

Only now when he passes by, the Zebra calls out, 'Qua-ha-ha! How's Kicking Tree?'

Somebody heard him, and came and told me so.

EGBERT, THE GRUMBLER

The Story of a Bright Young Camel

THERE was once a clever young camel called Egbert.
He was called Egbert because Egbert means 'terribly
bright', and nobody had ever met a brighter young
camel than Egbert. This doesn't mean that he was
clever in the same way as you or me. He didn't even

want to be. Indeed, he would have curled his lip and
screwed up his nose at the very idea, because he thought
other people very stupid. So did his mother and father,
his grannie and his grandpa, his auntie and his uncle,
and every one of his cousins. They all thought other
people very stupid. They often used to sing a song about

it; though sing is not a very good word to use. It would be far truer to say that they groaned the song, and simply snorted the chorus:

'Pooh! Every camel knows that you
Can't do half what he can do.'

And the very first thing Egbert learned to do was to grumble. Now your mother and mine never dream of teaching us how to grumble. We have to learn the best way we can, all by ourselves. And even then, they often and often say, 'Oh, please DON'T grumble!' But Egbert's mother was different.

She TAUGHT him to grumble. She would put her head down close to his, and grumble and groan and complain like billy-oh. Then she'd say, 'Now you try, there's a bad boy!' And Egbert would look up at the blue sky, and groan and moan as if he had a nasty tooth-ache, a terrible tummy-ache, and a most awful hump-ache, all at once.

This pleased his mother very much. It also pleased all his other relations. They said he sounded as if he was going to be the best grumbler they'd had in the family for years. So they began to give him other lessons.

His father taught him never to go down on his knobby knees without groaning dreadfully. Egbert had tough, leathery pads on his knees, so it didn't hurt him in the least to kneel down, but his father said well-brought-up camels never dream of waiting to see if something is going to hurt. They complain first, just in case.

And his grannie taught him to grumble hard at his

dinner, even if it was something he liked very much, dates, for instance.

And his grandpa taught him to complain very loudly every time somebody heavy rode on his back.

Then his auntie taught him to groan just as loudly if somebody quite light rode on his back.

And his uncle taught him how to tuck his head under his tummy and look as if he'd tied himself into a knot and then forgotten how to undo himself again.

And his cousins taught him how to scratch his left ear with his right back leg. And if you don't think this is much of a trick, just try it yourself.

But Egbert was so bright that he learned all this in less than no time. He also practised his grumbling till even his grannie said she'd never heard anything like it, and that it was a pleasure to listen to him. She said it made her think of the dear old song that went like this:

> 'Oh, the high-born camel is a lovely sight,
>   As he groans and moans with all his might.'

Now, one day a very rich lady called Mrs Brown happened to pass by, just as Egbert was saying some very awful things about having to do a little work. Mrs Brown stopped and listened to Egbert, and said it was a shame. Then she straightway bought Egbert, and said she'd take him home with her and see what a little kindness could do.

So Egbert set out on his travels over land and sea, feeling pleased inside, but looking very haughty outside.

It was a long, long way to Mrs Brown's home in England. And Egbert grumbled every inch of the way,

though nobody made him do any work at all, and he ate the best of beans and dates, and drank as much water as he could hold.

At last they came to Mrs Brown's home, and Egbert was turned out to pasture in a lovely green meadow, with a running brook at one end. Egbert gave one look round him. Then he threw back his head, screwed up his nose, and moaned and moaned.

He said he hated grass; it was too green and messy.

He said he hated running water; it was too fresh and cold.

He said he supposed he'd better try and find a bite to eat somewhere before he died of hunger.

And he stepped right over the hedge, and ate up all the rose bushes in Mrs Brown's garden.

The next day he ate up all the gooseberry bushes.

60

And the day after that he chewed up all the washing on the line.

And the day after that again, he stepped over the hedge once more, went down the road, and started to chew up the thatched roof of old Mrs Penny's cottage.

Old Mrs Penny was very angry. She said that Mrs Brown ought to feed the poor beast, so that he wouldn't have to go round eating other people's roofs. She said you'd only to look at Egbert to see how miserable he was and that she'd half a mind to tell the police. Here, Egbert groaned very loudly as if to say, 'Do, pray do!'

So Mrs Brown thought that perhaps Egbert would be happier if he had company; and she offered to sell him to Mr Joe Bates who kept a circus.

Mr Bates came and had a look at Egbert. And Egbert had a look at Mr Bates, and began to show off his grumbling.

So Mr Bates said he would buy Egbert just to oblige Mrs Brown. He said people paid good money to enjoy themselves at his circus, not to cry their eyes out listening to somebody like Egbert.

But as he rode home on Egbert's back, Mr Bates suddenly had a very good idea.

The very next day this notice, in very large letters, was printed in all the newspapers:

COME TO JOE BATES'S CIRCUS. COME AND SEE EGBERT, THE CAMEL WHO REALLY HAS THE HUMP! WHY GRUMBLE YOURSELF? COME AND LET EGBERT DO IT FOR YOU. ADMISSION ONE SHILLING. CHILDREN HALF-PRICE.

Well, Egbert was a great success. People came from far and near to see and hear him. He never did any hard work, and Mr Bates fed him on the best of dates and beans. You see, he soon found out that the more he fed Egbert, the bigger grew his hump. And that the happier Egbert was, the better he grumbled.

So twice nightly, as well as every Wednesday and Saturday afternoon, Egbert did all these things·

1. Knelt slowly down when Mr Bates made a clicking noise.
2. Got up again.

62

3. Tucked his head under his tummy and pretended to tie himself into a knot.
4. Slowly undid himself again till his head came back to its usual place.
5. Scratched his left ear with his right back leg, to slow music.

And grumbled all the time at the very top of his voice.

I am told that he even learned to groan a poem that began:

> *What is life, if full of care,*
> *You have no time to groan and glare.*

And I am also told that he always ended up his turn by snorting his favourite song:

> *Grumble, grumble, everywhere,*
> *Grumble near and far,*
> *You must really work at grumbling*
> *If you want to be a star.*

After seeing Egbert, people always came out and laughed and laughed and laughed.

And this, of course, is the very best way to end up any grumbling, isn't it?

SPIN, THE DUTCH SPIDER

Or, why they say in Holland, 'As Cross as a Spider'

THERE was once a clever young spider called Spin, who lived in a corner of a windmill in Holland. All day long the wind came blowing over the grey-green sea

and across the green polders; and clack – clack – clack-etty – clack, round and round sailed the great arms of the mill.

All day long inside the mill the miller and his sons

busily ground the golden corn into creamy-white flour. And high up in a dark corner of the roof Spin busily caught flies, and daddy-long-legs, and beetles, and ants, and moths, and anything else that came blundering into her silken web.

When evening came she walked on her eight legs all over her web, mending tears and holes with fine threads of silk that she spun as she went.

She also cleared out all the rubbish and litter. And then, only then, when everything was neat and tidy, would Spin go off to bed. Oh, she was a hard-working Dutch spider, I can tell you!

But work as she might, her web slowly grew thicker and thicker with the white dust that blew up and around every time the mill door opened and shut.

'Dear me!' said Spin to herself one fine day. 'It is about time that I treated myself to a nice new coat. This one is getting very tight. And my, oh my, how dusty it looks!'

So for two whole days Spin stopped catching flies, daddy-long-legs, beetles, ants, and moths. Then feeling much thinner, she hung upside down on her web. And she wriggled and wriggled, and heaved and heaved. And z-z-z-h! Her dusty old coat split and fell off. And there underneath was a brand-new coat.

Then Spin pulled and pulled. And out from their old skins came her eight clean legs, all at once. (And if you think this is easy, just try to pull both your arms out of your coat, not one after the other as you usually do, but both at exactly the same time.)

Well, there hung Spin, still panting, and proudly

peering at her lovely clean coat and legs. And at that very moment the mill door opened wide, and in poured the warm golden sunshine of the world outside.

'I'll run away,' said Spin suddenly. 'That's what I'll do. I'll run away from all this dust. I'll go and see the world in my nice new coat. I must, I must!'

And she spun a long, long streamer of silk thread. The wind caught it up and tossed it high in the roof. Then down it floated and out it sailed through the door and up and away.

Now for all her eight eyes Spin was very short-sighted. She couldn't see where her silk streamer had blown. So she sat quite still and waited. Spiders are very good at waiting.

By and by she felt a tiny tug from far, far away. She pulled gently at her end of the streamer. Then she waited once more. Then she pulled a little harder . . . and then harder still.

And suddenly she KNEW. Somewhere, out there in the sunshine, the other end of her streamer had caught on something – and was holding fast.

So the streamer was now a bridge, a fine silken bridge that led from her dusty web to the bright world outside.

Then Spin took a deep breath, and began to run on her nice clean legs along that silken tight-rope. It stretched and swayed as she ran. But it held. And out through the door, high over the heads of the miller and his sons, ran little Spin, out into the air and sunshine.

'Ouch!' gasped Spin. 'I can't say I like all this fresh air. Far too much of it! Oh, my goodness, far, far too much of it!'

And she blinked all her eight eyes and hurried on across her silken bridge. Presently, to her great relief, she felt something hard beneath her running legs. And there she was on a window-sill of the miller's house. And there too was the other end of her bridge, neatly caught round a handy nail.

'Thank goodness that's over,' said Spin. 'I must get inside or I'll catch my death of a cold in all this fresh air. Br-rr-rr! Whoever would think there could be such a lot of it!'

So she scuttled across the sill, squeezed through a crack in the window-frame, and stepped into the miller's parlour.

It was the tidiest, cleanest room you ever saw. Everything sparkled and shone; everything stood smartly in exactly the right place; and a neat little canary sang in a trim green cage near the sunny window.

'Hum!' said Spin. 'This looks a likely place.' But being a spider, she sat still in her corner and waited. Spiders never mind waiting to make quite sure.

By and by the door opened and in came the miller's daughter, Toje. She gave the canary clean seeds and water, and she cleaned out its trim green cage. Then she brushed, and dusted, and polished, and scoured, till everything in the parlour sparkled and shone even more than before.

And all the while Toje talked lovingly to the canary who twittered back as if he understood every word.

'Well! Well!' thought Spin. 'She seems to love that silly yellow bird. Yet, as far as I can see, he doesn't do a stroke of work. Just sits and sings and waits for his meals to be given to him. Doesn't even clean out his own cage if you please! Ah well, just wait till they find out how clever and useful I am.'

That night, when everybody else in the miller's house was fast asleep, Spin walked carefully all round the parlour. Then she settled on the place to spin her web. And all through the long dark night Spin worked and worked.

In the morning there it swung, high over the canary's trim green cage. It was a fine, three-cornered sheet of silk. In one corner was a little parlour, shaped like a tube. And from it hung a long overhead rope of silk that stretched to the farthest corner of the web.

'There!' said Spin proudly. 'How very nice it all looks!' And she crawled wearily into her little parlour to have a rest. But no sooner was she inside than the rope began to quiver and shake. 'A-ha!' said Spin. 'Here comes my breakfast, nice and early!' And sure enough, there, caught in the new web, buzzed an angry fly.

Well, by the time Toje came in to feed her canary, busy Spin had caught two flies, one daddy-long-legs, and a very ugly blue-bottle.

Suddenly Toje saw the web as it swayed gently over the trim green cage. 'Oh jé, jé, jé!' she cried, and dashed from the room.

'She's overjoyed!' said Spin solemnly to herself. 'She's never had a clever hard-working pet like me. She's gone to fetch the rest of the family to have a look at me.'

But Toje hadn't. She'd gone to fetch a brush, a brush with a very long handle. And, oh goodness, oh deary, deary me, she swept down Spin's new web, she swept down her neat little parlour, she swept down her overhead rope. Yes, she swept them all down, and then shook her brush out of the window.

'A spider!' she cried. 'A nasty spider! And in the best parlour too! Oh, jé, jé, jé!'

But she didn't shake Spin out of the window. At the very first touch of that horrid brush Spin spun a thread for her very life. She tucked in all her eight legs and down she fell on her thread, and lay motionless beneath a chair, pretending she was dead – very dead. But my, oh my, how cross she looked.

69

'The idea!' she thought angrily to herself. 'The very idea! Here I am, all dressed up in my nice new coat, as clean and tidy as any spider in Holland, and I'm not allowed in the parlour. Huh!'

And there she lay all day long, scowling hard, till it was dark once more.

Then she ran quickly to the door, squeezed under it, and found herself in a warm kitchen.

'Oh well, after all,' said sensible Spin, 'I suppose this is where the work is done.'

And she ran round and round to find a good place to make her home.

When morning came, there over the stove hung Spin's new web. And there in her new little parlour, with one foot on her overhead rope, waited patient Spin, all ready to catch her own breakfast.

Then in came the miller's wife to make the coffee. As she set the pot upon the stove, she caught sight of Spin's lovely web over the stove, shining in the morning sun. 'Heavens!' cried the miller's wife. And she picked up the stove brush, yes, the dusty old stove brush, and she swept down poor Spin's new web, her neat little parlour, and her overhead rope.

And again Spin spun a thread for her very life, tucked in all her eight legs, and fell down to the floor. And all day long she lay beneath a cupboard, pretending to be dead – very dead. But my, oh my, how very, very cross she looked. It is not amusing to work all night and then lie pretending to be dead all day, I can tell you.

And as the days went by poor Spin began to look crosser and crosser and crosser. For she was harried, and hunted, and chased, and worried, till it became quite clear that in all that shining spotless house there was no safe corner for a spider, no matter how clean and obliging.

The more Spin thought of this the angrier she grew. 'Do I ask them to feed me?' she grumbled. 'Or clean out my web? Or take me out for walks? No, no, and NO! I am sensible, quiet, and hard-working. I give no trouble at all. All I ask is to be left alone to catch the flies they say they hate so much. And what happens? They tear down my webs, my lovely silk webs and they say rude things about dirty spiders. Dirty! Oh, oh, oh!'

Spin simply scowled with rage. And from that

moment she thought only of how to escape from that clean unfriendly house.

One happy morning everything was ready. The parlour window stood open wide. High up, hidden behind the folds of the stiff red curtains, swung Spin's latest web. From it stretched a long thin thread. It stretched out through the window, out and out. Spin didn't know where the other end had caught. She didn't care. All that mattered was that it *had* caught on something out there, far, far away from the miller's house. It was Spin's new bridge to freedom.

'And now,' said Spin, 'I have just one more job to do.'

She spun another fine thread. Down she dropped on it till she was level with the canary's trim green cage.

And there she hung scowling most dreadfully.

The canary gave her one frightened look and screamed. 'Help – help – oh – help-p-p-p!'

In rushed the miller's wife and Toje. And round spun Spin on her rope, and she scowled and scowled and scowled. Yes, she scowled her fiercest, blackest scowls with all her eight angry eyes.

IT WAS TERRIBLE!

'Jé, jé, jé!' cried Toje.

'Quick! The broom! The brush! The mop!' roared the miller's wife. And they rushed to get them. But Spin didn't wait for them. She climbed up her rope, swung herself on to her silken bridge, and away she ran, far, far away to a safe place. And there she lived happily ever after.

But she went on scowling most crossly – just in case, I suppose. She also taught all her children to scowl. She must have done. For to this very day all Dutch spiders look very cross. And this, of course, is why people in Holland say, 'As cross as a spider' when they describe somebody very bad-tempered.

But between you and me and the windmill Spin's large family don't care a rap what anybody says. They go on catching flies, daddy-long-legs, beetles, ants, blue-bottles, and moths, and take the utmost pains to look as cross as possible.

JONES'S TITUS

TITUS JONES is not what you would call a handsome parrot. Indeed he is just plain grey all over. But old Mrs Jones, with whom Titus has lived these forty years, says 'handsome is as handsome does', and that you wouldn't find a nicer, chattier parrot, no, not if you searched from here to Africa and back.

Now I fancy Titus knows what Mrs Jones says. For he squawks and whistles and talks and sings all day long. He can also make a most remarkable noise that sounds as if he were tearing up calico. Mrs Jones is rather deaf. So she enjoys listening to Titus, even when he's pretending to rip up calico.

Titus lives in a fine large cage. But he only lives there because he likes it. He can undo the door with his strong beak and fly out whenever he pleases.

Sometimes he flies to the table near the window and perches there squawking 'Hullo! Hullo!' to the children going to school.

Then they shout:

> '*Oh, Jones's Titus,*
> *PLEASE don't bite us!*'

And Titus shrieks back:

> '*Okay, okay,*
> *Not today,*
> *Not today.*'

74

Sometimes he flies to the top of a tall bookcase and hides in a dark corner near the wall. Old Mrs Jones always knows he is there, but she calls out, 'Oh, my goodness, where's that Titus? Titus! Titus!'

And Titus screeches back 'Coo-ee,' or else growls like

75

a dog. It depends on how he feels. But Mrs Jones never worries. She knows he'll fly back to his cage when he wants something to eat.

On fine summer days, Titus sits on a wooden perch in the garden near the kitchen door where old Mrs Jones can keep an eye on him. She also takes care to fasten one end of a long thin chain to a ring round one of his legs. The other end of the chain is nailed to the perch so that Titus won't fly too far away. And when old Mrs Jones is doing this, I've noticed something most peculiar.

TITUS JONES ALWAYS GIVES A LONG SLY WINK! Mrs Jones doesn't seem to notice it. But I always do. And it used to puzzle me. When people wink, I like to know why. And now, at long last, I know. Yes, I know why Titus Jones winks. And a queer story it is, too, as you shall hear.

About three years ago a jackdaw built his nest in our church tower. A brisk, dapper, swaggering sort of bird he was, so we called him Swagger Jack. He wasn't particularly fond of us but he took a great fancy to Titus Jones. He would sit on Mrs Jones's fence and call, 'Clack! Clack!' till Titus noticed him. And then, my, oh my, how Titus would show off! He would squawk, shriek, whistle, sing, talk, and make his tearing-up calico noise as if he were fifty parrots rolled into one. And there Swagger Jack would sit, listening most admiringly.

'Oh, clack-clack!' he cried one day, when Titus had been showing off like billy-oh. 'Oh, Mr Jones, there's marvellous you are!'

76

'Not half! Not half!' squawked Titus, puffing out all his feathers. 'Titus Jones for ever! Good old Titus, that's me!'

'What a pity,' went on Swagger Jack sadly, 'what a shame those birds down in Lammas Wood won't believe a word I say!'

'Eh?' said Titus sharply.

'No, sir,' said Swagger very meekly, 'they just won't believe you can sing and talk like – er – THEM. They say you're nothing but a dicky-bird!'

'What!' shrieked Titus.

'Oh yes, Mr Jones,' said Swagger, 'they're an ignorant lot, I'm afraid. Why, they even say, "Old Titus Jones just sits in a cage, a'squawking for his meals", really they do.'

'What?' screamed Titus, and he made his most terrible noise. It was far, far worse than his tearing-up calico one. It sounded as if he were tearing up a whole road, telephone poles and all.

'But what I say is,' went on Swagger Jack, when Titus stopped to take a breath, 'what I say is, "seeing is believing". But there it is, more's the pity. They won't come and see you. And you can't fly down to Lammas Wood, of course.' And he sighed deeply.

'Can't! Who says I can't fly down to Lammas Wood?' roared Titus. 'Why, I'll go there this very minute.'

'A-aw!' said the jackdaw, and his eyes shone strangely. 'You can't rush off like that. People like you are missed at once. Why, you'd have half the village out searching for you. And it would be a pity if you had to come home in a hurry. For it's my belief, Mr Jones, those birds will want to make you King, yes, King of Lammas Wood. Yes, that's what they'll want to do, or my name's not Daw.'

'Hm!' said Titus. 'What's a king?'

'Sort of an eagle,' said Swagger Jack, 'only better, far more important.'

'Well – !' said Titus, very pleased indeed.

'And so,' said Swagger Jack quickly, 'we must plan things properly.' And he flew close to the perch and began to whisper very secretly.

Early next morning, old Mrs Jones came down as usual and pulled back the curtains and opened the window to let in the sweet morning air.

'Good morning, Titus,' she said. 'My, there's solemn you look!'

'King Titus!' muttered Titus, a far-away look in his eye.

'Titus the first, King of all Lammas.'

'Eh?' said old Mrs Jones. And hurried off to get his breakfast.

As she shut the door behind her, out flew Titus from his cage, and in through the open window flapped the jackdaw.

'Quick, up there,' said Titus. 'Your breakfast will be here in a moment. I am off, off to Lammas!' And with a great whirr of his grey wings, he shot through the window and across the garden.

'A-a-aw!' laughed the jackdaw. 'Oh, what a time I'm going to have!' He flew to the top of the tall bookcase and hid in the dark corner near the wall. And there he waited for his breakfast, his eyes shining greedily.

'Oh, my goodness,' called old Mrs Jones, as she came into the room. 'Now, where's that Titus? Titus! Titus!'

From the top of the bookcase came a hoarse growl, just like a dog – a dog with a very bad cold on his chest.

'Goodness!' said old Mrs Jones. 'Titus, you do sound queer.'

She fetched a stool and stood on it. In the dark corner she could just make out the jackdaw, his head turned to the wall, growling most huskily.

'Dear, dear! There's dull and poorly you look!' said old Mrs Jones. 'It's medicine for you today, Titus, my boy.'

She took away the nice tasty breakfast, and brought in a large dish of water into which she carefully measured three drops of blackest medicine.

'There, drink it all up, there's a good boy,' she said. 'You'll be better presently.'

And she closed the window, drew the curtains, and went out, shutting the door behind her.

'Poorly, am I?' croaked Swagger Jack savagely. 'Dull I look, do I? Medicine for me, is it?' And he fairly danced with rage.

He flew down, took one sip of the water, and shuddered all over. As he opened his eyes again he spotted something interesting on the table. It was a work-box. The lid was open, and in it shone some brass buttons, two or three thimbles, a pair of small scissors, and a long, shiny bodkin.

'Clack!' said Swagger Jack, the jackdaw. 'As my

poor dear pa always used to say, every cloud has its silver lining.'

When night fell, there in the dark corner on top of the tall bookcase, his head turned to the wall, slept Swagger Jack. He was very hungry, but very pleased. For close to his feet was a shining store of six bright buttons, three thimbles, a small pair of scissors, and a long, shiny bodkin.

And in the room above, old Mrs Jones stirred uneasily in her bed. She was very worried because Titus had behaved so queerly all day long, refusing to come down from the bookcase, and growling so hoarsely.

And what was happening down there in Lammas Wood? Yes, what had happened to Titus Jones who had flown away to become King of all Lammas?

Alas and alack! He was shivering and cowering in a

great oak tree, wishing and wishing he were safe at home.

All day long he had squawked and whistled and sang and talked, till he'd nearly burst. And not a bird, not a single bird had noticed him.

When he flew towards them they flashed off through the thick green leaves. He had called and coaxed and begged and scolded. Not a twitter, not a chirrup answered him. Yet he knew they were there, watching, mocking, and laughing. All the wood was full of their mocking murmurs.

So there he sat in the great oak tree and shouted, 'Coo-ee! Coo-ee!' just to keep up his spirits.

'Tu-whit! Tu-woo!' suddenly called a voice above him. And there blinking at him was a tawny owl. 'Stop that din!' he ordered. 'Why, rats and mice, if it isn't that noisy cousin of mine from down in the village!'

'Cousin?' said Titus.

'Yes, cousin,' snapped the owl. 'Like it or lump it. I'm your cousin, all right. What are you doing here, anyway?'

But before Titus had time to answer, he snapped again, 'Hungry, too, I suppose?'

'Very!' said Titus. 'Not a bite has anybody offered me all day long.'

'Offered you, indeed!' hooted the owl. 'That's good, that is! Here in Lammas Wood, dear cousin Titus, we have to work for our grub.' And he laughed again most rudely.

Then suddenly he stopped. 'Here, you go off home,' he said sharply, 'they'll go for you if you're still here in the morning.'

'Go for me?' whispered Titus.

'They'll get together,' said the owl, 'and they'll go for you. You might be able to manage them, a bird at a time, but a mob of them takes some tackling, believe me. I've had some.'

'But I can't go back till the morning,' said Titus piteously, 'the window won't be open.'

'Then just you stay where you are,' said the owl. 'But no noise, mind. I've got to have my rest. I'm on night work.' And he huddled close against the tree and fell fast asleep.

And there poor Titus perched in the growing dusk; and slowly the trees grew darker and darker; and one by one the faint mocking murmurs around him died away.

He thought of his beautiful cage and his supper and his dish of cool water; and most of all, he thought of kind Mrs Jones and the laughing children who called him 'Jones's Titus'. And he knew, deep down within him, that it was there that he belonged, that it was there that he was truly king, not here in this cold, dark, menacing wood.

Suddenly, on silent wings, the owl swooped down towards him. 'Hi!' he whispered. 'Here's your supper.'

Titus peered at it, and felt very sick. For there on the branch beside him, limp and still, hung a rat.

'I'll be back when it's light,' breathed the owl. 'Stay where you are.'

But when the chill quiet light of day came creeping into Lammas Wood, Titus Jones flapped his damp grey wings. 'Hurrah!' he squawked. 'Hurrah!' And off he flew, and waited for no one.

At half past seven exactly that morning, a wet, tired, bedraggled parrot flew in through Mrs Jones's open window. Five seconds later out tumbled a frightened jackdaw croaking, 'A-aw! A-aw!'

It was Titus Jones turning out Swagger Jack, neck and crop, with many a hearty shove and nip.

In rushed old Mrs Jones. 'Why, Titus,' she said, 'there's a sight you look! And my, oh my, there's hungry you seem!' And she almost ran to get his breakfast.

Then Titus Jones flew into his cage, and sang and sang with all his heart and voice. He sang all the songs he knew. He even made up a new one:

East, west, home's best.
And you can keep your woods
And all the rest.

And now you know why Titus Jones winks when old Mrs Jones chains him to his perch.

But of course Mrs Jones doesn't know that Titus wouldn't run away from home for all the nuts in Africa. And I'd rather you didn't tell her, please. It may upset her.

What's that? What about the buttons, the thimbles, the scissors, and the long, shiny bodkin?

Oh, old Mrs Jones's niece found them when she did the spring-cleaning. She told me so herself.

KLAAS, THE STONE-CUTTER

A Story from the Dutch East Indies

Now there was once a stone-cutter called Klaas, who worked hard all day long hewing stone from a great rock near his home. He was a fine strong man and very clever at hewing and chipping stone.

But in those days nobody paid much money even for the best of stone. So Klaas was poor, very poor.

One morning he sat down to eat his breakfast in the shade of the great rock. And he began to think how pleasant it would be if he were rich, very rich. He remembered a picture he had once seen in a book, a picture of a rich man in a tall silk hat, a coat with a fur collar and shiny leather boots. Klaas sighed, and said aloud, 'I wouldn't mind changing places with him for a bit, that I wouldn't!'

Now, some people think that Klaas, without knowing it, must have chosen an enchanted place to sit and think aloud like this. But others say no, it must have been exactly seven minutes to seven on the seventh day of the seventh month. For this, they say, is the most magic time in all the year to think aloud.

But whatever it was, the moment Klaas said these words – crack! There he was, in a tall silk hat, a coat with a fur collar, and shiny leather boots, climbing up the marble steps of a fine house.

Two servants, in red velvet suits, flung open wide the great carved doors. Bowing low, they asked if they should take his hat and coat.

'Certainly not!' said Klaas. 'The very idea!' and he proudly stroked his fur collar and rubbed his tall hat on his sleeve till it shone like glass.

'Breakfast is served,' said a third servant in a purple suit. He led Klaas into a grand room where a table was covered with plates and plates of good things to eat.

'Maybe this is a dream,' said Klaas to himself, 'so I'll waste no time.' And he drew up a chair and began to eat. The sun poured in through the open windows. But Klaas refused even to think of taking off his hat and coat. So by and by, of course, he began to feel warm, very warm indeed. Also his shiny leather boots began to pinch his hot feet.

It was then that he noticed a picture in a gold frame, hanging on the wall before him. It was a picture of a king of some distant land. He lay on a red satin couch; two black servants waved large feather fans over his head; he wore a thin silken gown; his feet were bare; and little fountains of water sparkled and splashed on either side of him.

'My!' said Klaas, feeling even hotter, 'I wouldn't mind changing places with him!'

And crack! There he was, his feet quite bare, in a thin silk gown, lying on a red satin couch. Two black servants waved feather fans over his head, and he could see the little fountains, splashing and sparkling in the sunshine.

But in spite of his bare feet, his thin silk gown, the feather fans, and the fountains, Klaas, the king, was hotter than ever before. For high overhead in the deep blue sky the sun blazed fiercely over all the earth.

'Say what you like,' said Klaas, 'it is only the sun who is truly happy and contented. There he shines, just pleasing himself, and not worrying in the least about scorching a king like me. I wouldn't mind changing places with him, that I wouldn't!'

And crack! There was Klaas, blazing away, high up in the deep blue sky.

'Well, well,' said Klaas, 'so now I'm the sun! This is a job after my own heart at last.'

And he shone so hard that the king got up from his satin couch, took off his silk gown, and sat down under one of the little fountains. The rich man tore off his hat, his coat, and his shiny leather boots. Away in the hills, little streams dried up and disappeared. Even the hard snow houses in far frozen lands began to melt and drip.

'Why!' said Klaas, the sun. 'This is glorious. I am lord and master over all.'

But as he said this, a great cloud came sailing between him and the earth. And shine as he might, his rays just flickered and failed. Then down from the cloud poured a torrent of rain. The king scrambled out from the fountain, the black servants hastily folded up their fans and raced off with the satin couch; the rich man put

on his hat, his coat and his shiny leather boots; the little streams began to trickle joyously down from the hills once more and all the thirsty earth drank and rejoiced.

'Hm!' said Klaas, the sun. 'That cloud certainly leads a cool, pleasant life. I think I'd enjoy changing places with him.'

And crack! There he was, sailing dark and cool across the sky.

'This is the life for me,' cried Klaas, the cloud. And he raced all over the sky and rained and rained with all his might; and the little streams grew deep and wide, and overflowed their banks. They surged down to the sea, carrying mud and stones and even trees before them. And all the earth seemed to bow and shake under the drenching rain.

Then Klaas, the cloud, roared in triumph, 'There is no end to my power and strength. Just watch me roll this great rock over.'

But though he rained and rained till he almost burst with rage, the great rock stood firm and took no notice at all of the rain beating on it.

Klaas, the cloud, grew suddenly quiet. 'Now, look at that rock!' he said to himself. 'There he stands and doesn't even notice my raging torrents. I wish I were he, so calm and strong and steady.'

And crack! There stood Klaas the rock, with the rain still streaming down his craggy sides. And though no one could hear him, of course, he laughed aloud at all the world, and told himself that now at least he was safe and stronger and more powerful than anybody, anywhere.

But as the sun rose the next morning, a stone-cutter came along. He carried a pickaxe, a chisel, and a strong hammer. And he set to work to hew stone from the sides of Klaas, the rock.

'Ouch! Ouf!' groaned Klaas. 'This man is even stronger than I am. In time he will hew me down to the very ground itself. Oh, if only I were a fine strong stone-cutter!'

And crack! There once more sat Klaas, the stone-cutter, quietly eating his breakfast in the shade of the great rock.

*Other Young Puffins which have been
especially designed for children under eight
are described on the following pages*

LUCKY DIP *Ruth Ainsworth*
Stories from the BBC's *Listen With Mother*. Seven of the ever-popular *Charles* stories are included. (Also available in Initial Teaching Alphabet edition.)

THE TEN TALES OF SHELLOVER *Ruth Ainsworth*
The Black Hens, the Dog and the Cat didn't like Shellover the tortoise at first, until they discovered what wonderful stories he told.

LITTLE PETE STORIES *Leila Berg*
More favourites from *Listen With Mother*, about a small boy who plays mostly by himself. Illustrated by Peggy Fortnum.

A BEAR CALLED PADDINGTON *Michael Bond*
MORE ABOUT PADDINGTON
PADDINGTON HELPS OUT
PADDINGTON AT LARGE
PADDINGTON ABROAD
Named after the railway station on which he was found. Paddington is an intelligent, well-meaning, likeable bear who somehow always manages to get into trouble. Illustrated by Peggy Fortnum.

THE HAPPY ORPHELINE *Natalie Savage Carlson*
The twenty little orphaned girls who live with Madame Flattot are terrified of being adopted because they are so happy.

FIVE DOLLS IN A HOUSE *Helen Clare*
A little girl called Elizabeth finds a way of making herself small and visits her dolls in their own house.

TELL ME A STORY *Eileen Colwell*
TELL ME ANOTHER STORY
TIME FOR A STORY
Stories, verses, and finger plays for children of three to six, collected by the greatest living expert on the art of children's story-telling.*

MY NAUGHTY LITTLE SISTER *Dorothy Edwards*
These now famous stories were originally told by a mother to her own children. Ideal for reading aloud. For ages four to eight.

* *A Young Puffin Original*

MISS HAPPINESS AND MISS FLOWER
Rumer Godden
Nona was lonely far away from her home in India, and the two dainty Japanese dolls, Miss Happiness and Miss Flower, were lonely too. But once Nona started building them a proper Japanese house they all felt happier. Illustrated by Jean Primrose.

THE STORY OF FERDINAND *Munro Leaf*
The endearing story of the adventures of the nicest bull there ever was – and it has a very happy ending.

MEET MARY KATE *Helen Morgan*
Charmingly told stories of a four-year-old's everyday life in the country. Illustrated by Shirley Hughes.

PUFFIN BOOK OF NURSERY RHYMES
Peter and Iona Opie
The first comprehensive collection of nursery rhymes to be produced as a paperback, prepared for Puffins by the leading authorities on children's lore. 220 pages, exquisitely illustrated on every page by Pauline Baynes.*

LITTLE OLD MRS PEPPERPOT *Alf Prøysen*
Gay little stories about an old woman who suddenly shrinks to the size of a pepperpot.

DEAR TEDDY ROBINSON *Joan G. Robinson*
Teddy Robinson was Deborah's teddy bear and such a very nice, friendly cuddly bear that he went everywhere with her and had even more adventures than she did.

THE MERRY-GO-ROUND *selected by James Reeves*
An unrivalled collection of verse. There are some for six-year-olds, and many for twelve-year-olds; most readers over nine will love them all.

THE ADVENTURES OF GALLDORA
Modwena Sedgwick
This lovable rag doll belonged to Marybell, who wasn't always very careful to look after her, so Galldora was always getting lost – in a field with a scarecrow, on top of a roof, and in all sorts of other strange places.

SOMETHING TO DO *Septima*
Suggestions for games to play and things to make and do each month, from January to December. It is designed to help mothers with young children at home.*

* A Young Puffin Original

PONDER AND WILLIAM *Barbara Softly*
Ponder the panda looks after William's Pyjamas and is a wonderful companion in these all-the-year-round adventures. Illustrated by Diana John.*

CLEVER POLLY AND THE STUPID WOLF
Catherine Storr
Clever Polly manages to think of lots of good ideas to stop the stupid wolf from eating her.

DANNY FOX *David Thomson*
Clever Danny Fox helps the Princess to marry the fisherman she loves and comes safely home to his hungry family.*

THE URCHIN *Edith Unnerstad*
The Urchin is only five years old – but already he has the Larsson family at sixes and sevens with his ingenious tricks and adventures.

LITTLE O *Edith Unnerstad*
Little O, the Urchin's little sister, is sometimes a bit sad that she has no younger brothers and sisters, but most of the time she is too busy to care.

LITTLE RED FOX *Alison Uttley*
Little Red Fox is adopted by kind Mr and Mrs Badger, but finds it hard to be as good as their own children.

THE PENNY PONY *Barbara Willard*
Life is never quite the same for Cathy and Roger after they find the penny pony in Mrs Boddy's shop. A delightful story for readers of six to eight.

MAGIC IN MY POCKET *Alison Uttley*
A selection of short stories by this well-loved author, especially good for five and six-year-olds.

GOBBOLINO THE WITCH'S CAT
Ursula Moray Williams
Gobbolino's mother was ashamed of him because his eyes were blue instead of green, and he wanted to be loved instead of learning spells. So he goes in search of a friendly kitchen. Illustrated by the author.

ADVENTURES OF THE LITTLE WOODEN HORSE
Ursula Moray Williams
To help his master, a brave little horse sets out to sell himself and brings home a great fortune.

* A Young Puffin Original